GAY EROTIC ROMANCE

BAREBACK
ON BOARD

DEXTER CHASE

About the Publisher

4Fun Publishing, a member of **BLVNP Incorporated**, A Nevada Corporation, 340 S. Lemon #6200, Walnut CA 91789, info@blvnp.com / legal@blvnp.com NOTE: Due to the highly emotional reaction of some people to works of erotic fiction, any email sent to the above address that contains foul language or religious references is automatically deleted by our anti-spam software and will not be seen. All other communications are welcome.

DISCLAIMER

Please don't be stupid and kill yourself. This book is a work of FICTION. Do not try any new sexual practice that you find in this book. It is fiction and not to be confused with reality. Neither the author nor the publisher or its associates assume any responsibility for any loss, injury, death or legal consequences resulting from acting on the contents in this book. Every character in this book is over 18 years of age. The author's opinions are not to be construed as the opinions of the publisher. The material in this book is for entertainment purposes ONLY. Enjoy.

Bareback On Board

Gay Erotic Romance

By: Dexter Chase

© Dexter Chase 2015

ISBN: 978-1-68030-286-8

Glossary of Naval terms used in this story:

Heads	-	Toilet/bathrooms
Make and Mend	-	Afternoon off
Brig	-	A ship's jail
Hook	-	An anchor worn on the sleeves of leading hand

Chapter 1

Twenty-four hours to go and the ship would be docking in Plymouth. The atmosphere on board was electric. Two thirds of the crew had been away for thirteen months so they were champing at the bit to get back to their loved ones. It should have only been eight months but thanks to Muslim fanatics they had remained in the Gulf to support the legitimate government as allies.

Peter de Salis was one of the other third. He had been on board for a few months learning his way around his department. He would remain in the ship for the long refit and work up with the new crew before the ship returned to South East Asia and he would move on to a new appointment.

Peter was a communications officer and stood a lot of mickey taking. Com officers had hyphenated names, or at least that appeared to be the case so he was always being told he was in the wrong branch. He was a lieutenant, head of his department at only 24 years old. He had been commissioned straight from school and therefore received his university education on the pay of a sub-lieutenant. He graduated at 21 with a first class degree, had been promoted to lieutenant straightaway, and became a communicator.

The captain believed that all of his officers should be able to run the ship if needs be, so at sea while making passage, officers like Peter would have to do a stint as second officer of the watch. A waste of time during the night watches, and that was why Peter, at two in the morning had been allowed to go down to his office to collect some paperwork he needed to do before the ship docked. He opened the door to the operations room and was about to turn on the lights when he saw a beam of light coming from the bottom of the door leading into his office. He brought out his cell phone, prepared to take some quick pictures if there was mischief afoot. No one should be in his office without his permission, and certainly not at two in the morning.

Peter opened the door and immediately took about a dozen pictures as he moved into the office and walked round the four young men that were there. They didn't move. They just looked at Peter with shocked expressions on their faces. Not surprising really. All four were naked. Two of them had their cocks up the arses of the other two.

"Watkins', I think you can remove your cocks from the Arnolds."

They did. Peter went round his desk and sat down.

"Do any of you know what punishment will be handed out at your Court Martials when these pictures are displayed?"

All four of them nodded their heads and looked terrified.

"I believe it is four years in a military prison followed by a dishonorable discharge. Let me see, you four are eighteen and nineteen so at 22 and 23 you will become civilians again after four years in prison. I imagine that will be a recipe to confirm the ruination of your lives. Would you agree with me?"

They nodded their heads more.

Adam Arnold was the baby of the four with regards to maturity and it showed. Tears were running down his cheeks. Four years seemed like an eternity to him.

Peter looked along the line of the four. These were the four communications ratings that had joined the ship with him on the same terms: remain with the ship during refit, go to sea for the shakedown with the new crew, and then be off for a new appointment. Under normal circumstance they could all have been leading ratings by the time of their new appointments. He saw Adam's tears and wanted to wipe them away then hug the boy and tell him everything would be alright.

"Charlie, how could you be so careless? Why didn't you lock the door?"

Charlie looked sick, "Didn't think anyone would be around at this time of night, Sir."

Peter shook his head. "Well, you are bloody fools, all four of you. Stand at ease."

The four had been standing rigidly at attention until this point. Peter had scoped them out while he spoke to them and realized they were probably the most stunning young men on the ship. He was as hard as he had ever been looking at them. Fortunately, he was wearing his uniform jacket which would hide the bulge in his groin if he stood up. They were also unique in the Royal Navy because they were two sets of identical twins. Charlie and Chris Watkins were nearly 20 years old, Adam and David Arnold were 18.

"When I leave, get dressed, return to your mess deck and go back to bed. You are not to mention this to another soul. Do you understand that order?"

All four men said, "Yes, Sir," in unison.

Peter stood up, took the papers from his desk that he came for and as he left his office just said, "Carry on."

Back on the bridge, Peter didn't do much work on his papers. He was deep in thought about the action he had witnessed, keeping him with a solid erection. At four, when he was relieved, he returned to his cabin still thinking about what the four lads did. The orgasm he had was ferocious just thinking about his four naked ratings.

***

The four ratings cleaned up and redressed. Charlie was the first to speak.

"This is weird. The boss should have immediately called the Master at Arms and had us thrown in the brig for the night before appearing in front of the commander in the morning."

"He didn't appear to be upset at what we were doing, only that we had been stupid not to lock the door."

"Yeah, that was a bit weird. Mind you, he is only a few years older than us, Charlie. Probably, he still thinks his cock is for pissing out of. Maybe he's gone straight to the wardroom for a large brandy."

Chris was making light of their predicament but Adam wasn't. He was still crying.

None of them had any sleep that night so they looked very jaded at breakfast the next morning. A messenger came up to them while they were eating, carrying a note for Charlie. He read it and looked at the others.

"It's from Lieutenant de Salis. We are excused from watch-keeping until after lunch and are to report to him when we finish breakfast."

The looks now were apprehensive, a great improvement from the terror last night.

As they stood in front of Peter's desk, they could see he had their individual files in front of him, looking more serious than he was.

"Chris, what do you think should have happened last night?"

A little unsure but he replied anyway, "I think you ought to have called the Master at Arms, Sir, and had us thrown in the brig."

"David, what do you think I am going to do now?"

David looked sick, "What Chris said you should have done last night."

"Good answers. Chris is quite correct and because I didn't, you are right as well, David."

The looks of terror were back. Four years in prison, they all shuddered.

"Stand at ease and listen very carefully. This is going no further. No one, other than us five, will ever know about this provided certain conditions are met."

Adam totally disintegrated. His sobs were heart-rending and his brother had to cuddle him for ages before he calmed down.

Charlie spoke for all of them.

"Whatever conditions you set, Sir, will be ok with us. We will do anything you want forever if we can remain as we are."

Peter knew now that the year in refit was going to be his best year ever. He was married to the Navy, hopefully until compulsory retirement, but the thought of a whole year with four gorgeous mistresses to satisfy his sexual needs was marvelous.

"Very well, Adam, you had better remain here for now. You three resume normal duties. I'll inform you of any changes to your routine."

The three left and Peter stood, moved round his desk and to Adam's surprise, he was taken into a hug.

Peter stroked the boy's back as he held him and spoke quietly to him, "I don't want to see any more tears my lovely boy. Everything is going to be alright now. Go straight to a heads and wash your face. We don't want anyone else to see that you have been crying, do we?"

Adam looked into Peter's eyes and was surprised to see so much compassion and concern.

"No, Sir, and thank you so much."

Very quietly, Peter spoke again as Adam was leaving, "Prison is no place for someone as beautiful as you."

Adam hesitated, wasn't sure he had heard correctly and continued, thinking about what Peter had said, 'He did say I was beautiful.'

Mid-morning break and the four sat together for coffee. Adam told the other three exactly what happened in Peter's office after they left.

David almost whispered his comment.

"Do you think the boss is gay?"

Charlie, always the extrovert jumped in then.

"Well, I'd sleep with him any time if he is. I think he is a DDG."

The others laughed.

"I guess he is, isn't he?" that Chris thought the same as his brother about everything was not unusual so his comment wasn't either. Their first comment about the boss when he had joined was that he was drop dead gorgeous, and of course, the fact that he was so young didn't hurt their case either.

"Well if he is, I hope he has a big cock for me to get hold of while I'm fucking him."

That set them all off. David came back on that one.

"Huh, it doesn't matter if he has a big one or not. My guess is that it's your arse that will be getting reamed out, not his."

Charlie grinned.

"Well, I may prefer to be on top, but to get him into bed I'd happily take his man rammer if he has one. When we were in shorts he never appeared to show anything, but who would in uniform shorts? He could have 12 inches and you wouldn't know."

"Ah, that's just wishful thinking on your part, David."

That was it. Peter needn't have any worries about his intentions towards these four. They would all be delighted to go to bed with him.

***

The Bay of Biscay was like a mill pond as they sailed through it giving the ship's company a chance to spruce up the outside and the ship was dressed overall as they entered Plymouth Sound. The Royal Marine Band was playing on the helicopter deck and the whole of the ship's company manned the side in dress uniform.

Peter had inspected all of his communicators before allowing them on deck.

"I am very proud of all of you today. Try not to lose your caps over the side when three cheers are sounded."

They all laughed and Peter continued, "I know two of you are remaining behind for a fortnight until the others return so the rest of you enjoy your leave and if you are re-appointed, good luck in your next posting. The refit crew I will see in two weeks' time."

That was it for Peter's division. There would be a cocktail party in the wardroom for the officers' wives and girlfriends that would come on board and then all but a few seamen officers would go on leave and re-assignment, or return as the refit crew to work with the dockyard crews. Peter was staying on board until he could find a flat to rent for a year. He didn't want to stay in the wardroom at the Naval Base because that would be too restrictive and he had nowhere to go for his leave.

He went ashore the next morning to hit all the local estate agents and let them have details of his requirements. A spacious, one-bedroom flat in the Barbican with good views, if possible, was his wish. Money wouldn't be a problem. A bachelor lieutenant was well-paid by civilian standards.

Luck smiled on him the second day of looking. The flat was on the first floor above a curio shop, right in the heart of the Barbican, with good views across the sound and into the yacht basin. The whole was very pleasing: old world charm, beamed ceilings, a good-sized reception room, and a bedroom with a queen-sized bed. The kitchen was compact but adequate and despite it being nearly 100 years old, the modernization had given him a decent bathroom with a large shower stall to compensate for no bath, which Peter hated anyway. He took it and was pleased with the discount he got for a long let.

Peter moved in for his two weeks leave and explored all the restaurants and bars in the area. The plan was to keep his uniforms on the ship, his cabin was still usable for that, and he would go back and forth in civvies or 'mufti,' as the navy called it.

Coming to the end of his leave, Peter did a risk assessment exercise in his head. In the two weeks of his leave he had seen no other naval personnel that he knew. Most of the ship's company that would be on board for the refit didn't know him because he had not been on board very long. Most of the officers and senior NCOs would live ashore with their wives and he didn't imagine that there would be many wandering down to the Barbican during the week. He might need to be a little careful at weekends. So, if he invited any of his four naughty boys here he would almost certainly get away with it if he ever decided to take any of them out to a bar or restaurant. He wasn't looking for anything permanent with any of the four, which simply wouldn't be practical, so he could be as naughty as he liked. They wouldn't object since he saved them from a long prison sentence. He wasn't especially kinky but he did want to try a few things that a normal boyfriend probably wouldn't let him get away with. He bought a douche and loads of lubricant. He also bought a punishment paddle and a cock gag from a sex magazine online and they had been delivered. Using material bought locally, he made a set of ankle and wrist cuffs with reasonable lengths of cord on each. The final thing he bought was a small car to potter around in. He registered it with the dockyard police so he could drive into work each day. If one of his boys was with him he could always pass it off as having picked them up as he drove in. He thought he had all the bases covered now so when the boys came back on board after their leave, he could send for them all together.

Chapter 2

"Good morning boys. Did you all have a good leave?" was Peter's welcome to his four juniors after their leave.

Nods and verbal 'yes's' confirmed that.

"Alright, relax. This is going to be our routine for the next year. I have checked all of your docs and I think we can use slack periods to get you ready to sit the exams for leading hand while you are on board. You will then, if I recommend you, pick up your hooks when you are time served for that advancement. Do all of you want that?"

All yes, so Peter continued, "Now, your involvement with each other. Are you fuck and suck buddies or is there something deeper in any of your relationships other than being brothers?"

The four of them looked at each other in shock. Where was the boss going with this one? No one answered for long enough so that Peter jumped in again.

"Ok, let me put it this way. Chris and Charlie, do either of you have any emotional tie with Adam and David?"

"Oh no, Sir," was Charlie's quick reply. "We just enjoy sex together."

"Ok, incest is only a word in my vocabulary, the morals of it don't worry me so be honest, are any of you involved sexually with your brothers?"

'Where the fuck is the boss going with this?' was a common thought.

A few blushes and they all admitted that they had all fooled around together, giving mutual blowjobs.

"I blow David sometimes, Sir, but neither of us penetrates the other."

"Chris and I are the same, Sir."

Peter was grinning now.

"Ok, the reason for the third degree is this. I am married to the navy, but for the next year I would like four mistresses. You four are my candidates. Most nights I would like to take one of you home to spend the night with. If I am feeling a little kinky, I might on occasion want to take two of you together. Do any of you object to that?"

Charlie, the brash one answered for all four. He gushed out, "Fuck no, Sir, you can have me anytime you like. I think you are really hot. I'm normally on top but you can have my arse as well."

The others were grinning now and put their 'yes' votes in as well. Peter was delighted.

"Ok, you know we would all be in the deepest shit possible if this gets out so please, don't go out getting drunk and upset the apple cart will you?"

"No Sir, we don't want to go to prison that's for sure."

"The last thing then, when there is no one else in earshot of us I'd like you to call me Peter, but please, don't use my first name in front of other personnel.

Four very happy, young com guys went back to work. They wondered who was going to be first to experience a night of sex with the boss. They found out at lunchtime. Peter asked Adam if he would like to join him for dinner and stay the night.

"Oh yes please, Sir."

"Good, change into civvies when you finish, bring your toilet gear with you and meet me outside the main gate. Don't bother to shower. We'll do that together in my flat. I'd like to pamper you."

Both men laughed and Adam almost bounced out of Peter's office.

Trial operation worked like clockwork. Just out of sight of the main gate, and because neither of them had showered they were first ashore and Peter picked up Adam with no problem. When they were in Peter's flat, Adam looked quite nervous. Peter spun him round so that they were face to face and then kissed him on the lips. Not a heavy one, just sufficient to let Adam know everything was ok.

"Just relax, Adam. I want you to enjoy what we do here because I think you are such a beautiful guy, even if I am a bit of a sex hound."

"I'll be alright, Peter, it just feels a little strange you being my boss."

Peter kissed him again.

"We'll soon get used to each other and I promise I'll try to make the sex good for you. Let's go and shower shall we? I want to give you douches as well so that we don't have any disasters when I make love to you."

Adam nodded and followed Peter to his bedroom. They stripped while watching each other, and Adam tried to match Peter's action. Peter was watching Adam all the time so that when they were both naked, he was sporting a nearly erect cock.

Adam wasn't because he was nervous. But that changed quickly as he looked at Peter. His foreskin was about halfway back on the glans and as he came to full erection it finished its journey. Adam gulped. It was a very impressive piece of man rammer. It wasn't the 12 inches Charlie had joked about but Adam guessed it must be 10 inches with a nice thickness.

"Oh gosh, Peter, that is very big."

Peter looked at Adam's that had now come to full erection as well. It was about five inches and circumcised.

"Yes, but yours is like the rest of you, beautiful."

The sight brought tears to Peter's eyes.

"I know I have seen you naked before, but now that I can really look at you I can't believe how lucky I am to have you here. You really are a beautiful boy, Adam."

Adam blushed but he was pleased that Peter admired him so much.

Peter was scoping out this boy as he talked. Adam was three or four inches shorter than him but the body was perfect. The pecs and abs looked as though a little work had been done on them, or he was very lucky with his build. He had unruly, mid-brown hair and none other than on his head, at the base of his penis, and under his arms. Peter had to remind himself that he mustn't get emotionally involved with this boy. There simply was no future for them.

They went for their shower and Peter made the douche as funny as he could before washing his beautiful boy. He deliberately paid special attention to the bottom because he knew he was going to rim that cute butt for a long time before he entered it. He shouldn't have a problem entering it because he remembered how big the other twins were and Adam had one of their cocks in his arse the first time Peter had seen them. Both of them maintained an erection during the shower and Peter would've normally played to orgasm, but he wanted Adam to be really horny this first time hoping it would help him relax and enjoy the sex more. They went to bed and Peter had Adam on his back, arms at his side, his legs a little way apart.

"You don't have to do anything this time, Adam. I just want you to let me do all the work to show you how incredibly sexy I think you are."

Adam was already sliding off to a new world. No one had ever said such nice things to him as a prelude to sex.

Peter started kissing the boy as he let his hand wander over his torso. He slowly went lower with his mouth until he was licking and kissing the nipples. They were small, and even when they were hard were only about an eighth of an inch long. He nibbled them as well making Adam gasp and shudder. He went further down until he reached the cock. A little lick of the head and then he continued down the shaft to the balls which he took in his mouth for a thorough swabbing while he used a slicked-up hand to play with Adam's cock. He worked the cock and balls carefully because he didn't want Adam to cum yet, then back to the lips after a little while to give Adam a chance to calm down.

"I think I could leave the other three alone, Adam, and just have you here every night because you are just amazing. If there was any future for us I probably would make you my partner."

Adam was reeling with that confession. He wouldn't have any objection to that at all. This man was taking him to places he had never been before.

"I want you to roll over on your tummy, come up on your knees, and open your legs wide. Keep your shoulders on the bed."

Adam did, wondering what was going to happen now.

Peter got between Adam's legs and looked at the view. He gently touched the cheeks and then started stroking them. The anus was a delight to look at. He used his hands to spread the cheeks more and leaned in to lick the hole. Adam nearly went through the wall.

"Oh God, Peter, what did you do?"

Peter was laughing almost too hard to speak so he rolled Adam back and lay down beside him.

"I am starting to make love to your bottom. I may take the remainder of the night to do it. Has no one ever rimmed you before?"

Adam shook his head.

"No, but it is pretty sensational. Would you like me to roll over again?"

Peter nodded. He couldn't believe how innocent this boy appeared to be, but he had seen him over his desk with a cock in his arse. The two images didn't meld at all. After another very passionate kiss, he went back to playing. He rimmed Adam for a while before spreading him more and trying to tongue-fuck him. Too much for Adam, he had a massive orgasm. Peter rolled him onto his back and licked up any cum that was left before taking a towel to clean up the quantity on his bed. Then he started again until he had Adam gasping. He moved back between the boy's legs with his container of lube. He worked a couple of fingers into his love tunnel and as he felt it relax, lubed his cock. He positioned himself, lifting Adam's legs and bending them to enter one very cute butt.

No visible pain on entry so Peter eased some more into his lover.

"That feels so good, Peter, you can keep going."

Not without experience, Peter was almost overcome by this boy. He went in all the way, apologizing when he saw the spike of pain as he went over the second barrier. He then fucked his lover slowly and deeply for ages. Eventually, there was nothing more he could do to stop his own orgasm so he sped up and was pleased that Adam had another massive orgasm before he followed suit. Peter almost shouted out with the pleasure of his orgasm. He couldn't remember ever having such a ferocious one. It felt like someone had squeezed his balls hard. He fell forward and sideways remaining inside his lover.

He kissed Adam and wanted to say things that he couldn't imagine to be true. This boy was exquisite as a lover. He was sure that even though David looked the same, he wouldn't engender the same feelings in Peter as Adam had.

When he had softened too much to remain in his new love, Peter slid out and then pulled Adam into a cuddle.

"Ok, Lover?"

Adam came back to earth very slowly.

"Oh yes, Peter, no one has ever made love to me like that. It's the most thrilling experience I have ever had."

Peter kissed him again and replied, "I'm so pleased because that goes double for me."

They lay stroking each other for some time before Peter spoke again, "Would you like to go out for dinner?"

Adam nodded, realizing he had not eaten since lunchtime.

"Let's have a quick clean up then. There is a nice little restaurant just along the road. We can eat there tonight and have a drink at the bar while they fill our order."

Adam liked the sound of that. If he ate ashore with the boys it would likely be a McDonald's or KFC. This sounded much more sophisticated.

Sitting at the bar, Adam had the same drink as Peter even though he had never tried a brandy/dry ginger before.

"Mmm, this is good."

Peter laughed. He was so happy to be with this boy.

"Yes it is. It's a wardroom regular. At cocktail parties, the stewards always walk around with jugs of gin, tonic, and horse necks. They just add Angostura bitters to the brandy and dry. No need to go to the bar then for refills."

Adam thought that was neat.

When they sat down, Peter ordered wine with their meal. Again, Adam thought it was great.

"Does your family have a lot of money, Peter?"

"What made you ask that, Adam?"

"Well, you have quite sophisticated tastes, don't you? So I suppose it came from money."

"No money, Adam, just a good education and then Dartmouth, the Royal Navy College for my rounding off as an officer."

Adam nodded and got on with his food. Back to the flat after dinner and Peter stripped down to his underpants.

"If I do this I don't need to do much laundry."

Adam laughed.

"Yes, we do the same thing at sea. Sit around the mess in our underwear."

Peter replied to that, "It's a good thing I'm not in your mess then because if I was I'd be permanently hard."

They sat on the sofa wrapped around each other and watched the international news on TV. It was still quite early when Peter suggested they went to bed.

"I would love to go 69 with you before falling asleep."

Adam grinned, "Oh good. I want to get my hands on your cock, it is gorgeous."

Teeth were cleaned and they fell into bed, kissed for a few minutes then swiveled round for a mutual blowjob. Both had mouthfuls of cum before they curled up to sleep. Adam spooned Peter and both of them slept soundly.

They wakened later at the sound of Peter's alarm. Peter came awake, cuddling his boy and sighed with pleasure. How he would love to do this every morning.

"Coffee, fruit juice, cereals, they are your only choices mid-week."

"All three please, Peter."

They sat at the breakfast bar looking at each other and Peter spoke first, "Was that alright last night, Adam?"

"Oh yes, Peter, that was heavenly. You are a wonderful lover."

"I would like to do that with you every night, Adam, but it would only lead to problems. We don't have a future together."

Tears came to Adam's eyes.

"I know. I shouldn't have fallen in love with you so easily."

"I'm sorry, Adam. I may take your brother and the other twins quite regularly, but I'm not sure I can with you."

Adam wasn't stupid. What Peter said was the truth. There was no future for them.

Back on board, David, Charlie, and Chris started the third degree.

"I'm sorry. I don't want to talk about it."

The three looked at each other wondering what the hell happened. Adam looked so sad. Had the boss been awful to him? David tried to coax something out of him. By mid-morning Adam couldn't take anymore. They were all working in the same compartment and Adam caved in to get some peace.

"If you must know, it was the most amazing experience of my life. Peter is an exquisite lover but I won't be going back there very often because he is falling in love with me, and I am in love with him as well."

He burst into tears and clung to his brother.

"We don't have a future together, David, so Peter thinks that we shouldn't see each other very frequently. What am I going to do?"

They were all shaken up by the depth of feeling that Adam had for their boss after only one night.

It was a very quiet compartment for the remainder of the morning and it didn't get much better in the afternoon. They did get a load of work done though, and when Peter inspected it at the end of the day, he was very pleased.

"Do this very often and I'll give you guys a load of make and mends."

The boys laughed. The three were watching how Peter and Adam reacted to one another. They realized it was uncomfortable for both of them. The look in Peter's eyes when he looked at Adam confirmed what Adam had said. It made them all gasp.

Peter didn't take anyone home with him that day. He was just too upset. Falling in love was not part of his game plan with these four sexy young men.

Sitting with a drink after he had made his dinner, Peter came to a decision.

'I can't get depressed about this. Whatever way I play this, I won't have a future with Adam. Peter tried to convince himself that this was the case.

The next day, he decided to take Chris home with him. He was going to get a little raunchy this session, but he would save his most wicked moves for Charlie because he was the extrovert in the group.

Chapter 3

Adam was most upset when Chris quickly changed into civvies after work and headed out of the mess while everyone else went for showers.

"You're going with Peter today, aren't you?"

Chris couldn't look at Adam. He just mumbled, "Yes. I have to, don't I?"

Peter picked him up clear of the dockyard gate and drove home. Chris was very quiet and Peter kept casting glances across to him, "A penny for your thoughts, Chris."

"I felt uncomfortable leaving the mess because Adam knew where I was going."

Peter blushed then and tried to sound as though he had no idea why.

"Why would that affect you? I thought we had agreed that you would all grace my bed at different times, or even together."

Chris felt awful about this.

"Come on, Sir, don't make this more difficult. We know that you and Adam really gelled. He knows that there is no future for you both together and he's really upset about it. Now, we are all uncomfortable at the thought of coming to you for sex."

Peter slumped over the wheel a little.

"Ok, you're right. We both understand that a long-term relationship isn't possible. The only way I can think of for us to get over it is to avoid each other as much as we can. If I keep taking the rest of you to bed, I'm hoping that it will make it easier. I have no doubt I will take Adam again because of what developed between us so quickly. But quite honestly, it isn't going to do either of us any good."

At the flat as they stood facing each other in Peter's bedroom, Peter briefed Chris about what was going to happen.

"We are both going to have a douche before we shower. We can pamper each other in the shower and then when we are really horny, we go to bed and see what happens. I assume you are normally a top from what I saw that night in my office."

Chris nodded, watching his boss and wondering what was

coming.

"I am as well but for today, I think we can both be a bottom for one session and then a top for another."

Chris looked down at Peter's groin. No one had discussed the size of his man rammer so Chris was wondering if it was a big one. Peter saw the look and laughed, "I have the advantage having already seen you naked and erect. Want to even the score?"

Chris relaxed a little and grinned, "Yes please, Peter."

"Well, go ahead then."

Chris loved it. Undressing the boss was fun. What he uncovered wasn't though. Chris sat back on his haunches as Peter came to full erection

"Oh fuck, that will split me in two if you plant that in my arse."

"No, it won't. I promise I will open you up and lube you well before I plant my little brain in you."

Chris had an incredible body. His abs and pecs were, quite obviously, obtained in a gym. Coupled with the rest, he was instant erection material and Peter had no problem on that score. The appendage gave him a little cause to worry. He undressed Chris and played with him long enough to get him an erection as well.

The cock was very thick and only an inch or so shorter than Peter's so he knew he would feel that going in. David and Adam had taken it regardless of its size so he should be able to as well.

They showered together following the same routine as he had done with Adam. When they got to bed Peter made a suggestion, "Why don't I make love to you first? Then we can have dinner and afterwards we can reverse roles."

Chris thought that was fine.

'I'm going to make it as good for Chris as I can, even if I don't have the same feelings for him as I do for Adam,' was Peter's thought as he started on this new boy.

The result was very similar. Peter had rimmed him because with his gym-trained body, Chris had a spectacular butt. Peter took a long time to open him up knowing that he wasn't used to taking cock. After two very intense orgasms, Chris knew what had made Adam so enthusiastic about Peter's lovemaking skills.

"Crikey, Peter, I can understand Adam's feelings now. I'm

definitely a top, but that was pretty spectacular."

Peter grinned.

"Well, we do our best. Come on, let's clean up and you can watch me demonstrate my culinary skills."

Chris sat at the breakfast bar with a beer and watched Peter put together a very good meal.

"You're a pretty handy guy to have around, Peter, aren't you?"

Peter laughed.

"I was a poor student so I had to economize all the time at university, doing my own cooking was the best way for me to do that."

Chris was surprised. Peter spoke with an upper class accent so he thought he came from a wealthy family, and said so. Peter laughed.

"I should have been so lucky if we were. My dad drives a lorry and my mum works in a factory. I have five siblings and we all crammed into a council house. I had to pay my way through my A levels and university so I worked every hour I could outside of my study time."

Chris was impressed. They sat and chatted after dinner until Peter thought it was appropriate to go back to bed for more sex.

"Can I really take charge of you and do what I like?"

This sounded interesting so Peter said, yes.

Chris planned that if he got the go ahead to be dominant, he was going to spank his boss for causing Adam to fall in love with him.

"We were all upset that you were so good for Adam so I'm going to punish you before I fuck you."

Peter was tickled by his assertiveness. He expected something like this from Charlie but not Chris. Then it clicked.

"You crafty bugger, you aren't Chris, are you?"

"No Peter, I'm Charlie. Even David and Adam can't tell the difference between us unless we speak, but I can easily sound less assertive so that I can be Chris. Now, I want you over my knees for a good spanking."

He was grinning and Peter could see the funny side as well. He just hoped he would still be grinning after Charlie had finished. He also hoped that Charlie would realize he could be in for some real pain and humiliation if he went over the top.

Charlie did know that there was a line to be drawn, so he only made Peter uncomfortable by spanking him but he didn't make them hard enough to bruise. He didn't make so much love to Peter either. He opened him up fairly quickly and fucked him doggy fashion. Peter had no idea that his prostate was so sensitive, or maybe Charlie was a master at his art. He fucked Peter as much as he could in the doggy position, making sure he pressed on the prostate every entry as he long-stroked him. The resulting orgasm was pretty spectacular for both men. Peter's was enhanced by the tingle in his bottom from the spanking. They hadn't kissed up to this point so Peter changed that. He rolled onto his back after Charlie withdrew and pulled him in to administer a very passionate kiss.

"That was pretty spectacular, Charlie. I might let you do that again."

Charlie was very pleased. He had enjoyed Peter fucking him, but he was definitely a top and this very sexy boss had been very exciting.

"I don't really know how you rate as a top, Peter, because the only other person who has fucked me is Chris, and that was just for experimentation. But as a bottom you are bloody exciting."

Charlie then realized he had let the cat out of the bag. He had told Peter that he and Chris had never done anal together, but Peter didn't appear to notice.

"You are pretty good yourself. That was very satisfying. I didn't expect it to be that good. I was more curious since you have a quite spectacular cock."

Charlie thought that a lot of Peter's attractions as a lover was what he said as much as what he did. He would love to be a fly on the wall when he made love to Adam to see how much better he was with someone that he was in love with.

Then it was time to sleep and resume normal business.

The next day, Chris and David quizzed Charlie about his night, and Charlie was full of it, giving up every detail.

"Fucking the boss after I had spanked him was great. He is without doubt the best fuck I have ever had."

"Thanks very much. Don't come running to me for anymore then, will you?"

That was a very pissed off David. Adam had said nothing until curiosity was killing him.

"Why did you spank Peter, and did you hurt him?"

Charlie looked belligerent as he replied, "I spanked him because he made you fall in love with him and that was stupid. He knew that couldn't go any further."

"We don't choose who we fall in love with, Charlie. The chemistry was there from the go. Both of us realized it even before we went to bed together. I hope he will ask me to sleep with him again. I've decided that I can handle our parting next year, even if I do fall deeper in love with him. I just want to spend time in his arms."

David gave him a hug, "My brother, the incurable romantic."

They all laughed and got on with their work.

During the next couple of weeks, Peter took David and Chris to bed. He wanted to show both of them how good he was and as another bottom boy for Chris, who was the spitting image of his brother, David got star treatment. Peter's comment afterwards summed up his attitude completely.

"You are spectacularly sexy, David, the same as Adam, but there is just something else with Adam that makes me love him."

"I know, Peter, I wish things could be different for you both."

Peter had spent two miserable weekends by himself. He had rented a dinghy a couple of times and sailed solo in the sound, but it hadn't brought him any joy. He had eaten alone in his flat and taken long walks on the Hoe and round the Barbican, but despite how interesting and vibrant the area, he had remained miserable. On the third Friday of the refit he sent for Adam in the middle of the afternoon.

Adam entered Peter's office looking very apprehensive. What had he done, or what did the boss want him for?

"You wanted to see me, Sir?"

"Yes, come in Adam, sit down."

They looked at each other and both could see the sadness in the other's eyes.

"You aren't very happy, Adam, are you?"

"No, Sir."

"I'm not either so I have two suggestions, and as they affect you I'm going to give you the choice. The suggestions are based on the premise that whatever choice you make, it is done with the knowledge that in about twelve months at the longest we are going to be compulsorily parted."

Adam nodded his understanding.

"Suggestion one. I ask for you to be reappointed straightaway instead of doing your second year on this ship. Suggestion two, we resume our relationship and live with the consequences when we get our next appointment."

Adam looked at Peter to be sure he was serious, and then he nearly flew round the desk, jumped into Peter's lap, and in between sobs and kisses managed to tell him, "Second suggestion, Peter. I'm dying a little everyday seeing you and not being able to touch."

Peter grinned. "In that case, you had better get your request for a weekend leave to me in the next five minutes so that I can get it to the duty regulator with the excuse that it got lost on my desk."

Peter signed the rather soggy request form. The tear stains wouldn't be too obvious by the time he got it to the Master at Arms' office.

David and the other twins were in no doubt that Peter had seen sense, when Adam packed a weekend bag and had a grin plastered on his face from ear to ear.

"I'll see you all on Monday morning," was his parting shot as he scurried out the door about ten seconds after work finished for the day.

They managed to get into Peter's flat before Adam almost buried Peter in kisses.

"I love you so much. I know I'll die when our new appointments come through but it will be worth it for a year with you."

Peter knew this was total madness. No good could possibly come from it, but he felt the same as Adam. Their lovemaking was almost heart-stopping in its intensity and Peter reduced Adam to tears of joy three times before they slept.

The next morning, two very hungry men sat down for a full breakfast, continually looking at each other and grinning.

"I love you so much."

"I love you more."

"Impossible."

Adam giggled, "I don't think anything is impossible with you. Can we go back to bed?"

So they did. After two more draining orgasms, they lay in each other's arms stroking each other.

"How often can we do this, Peter?"

"How about, every night you aren't on duty and during weekends?"

Adam's eyes widened as he gasped out, "Do you mean that?"

"Yes, I mean it. I know this is madness, Lover, but I really do love you so much."

It was lunchtime when they fully surfaced, showered, and dressed. Peter took his lover out for lunch to a quiet little restaurant near the Hoe, with nice views over the Sound. The season was over so there weren't a lot of people around.

"We'll have to think of things to do and places to go at weekends, Adam. We can't just lie in bed and make love all the time."

Adam pouted but had a sparkle in his eyes, "Spoilsport."

That was no contest. Peter looked around to make sure no one was looking and leaned across the table to kiss Adam. The shocked look had Peter curled up laughing.

Peter had lost count of how many times they made love that first weekend, but he knew they hadn't spent much of it out of bed. And even out of bed they didn't put any clothes on so that they could touch each other in special places all the time if they felt like it.

"You're insatiable, Adam Arnold. You'll turn me into a sex maniac if you keep this up."

"Ooh lovely. Will you rape me then instead of making love to me?"

"What a good idea. Of course, I'll have to tie you up and punish you first."

"Oh yes, beat me and then fuck me to death."

Peter laughed again. He was doing rather a lot of that this weekend.

"When I knew I was going to have free rein with four gorgeous men for the next year, I bought a few bits so that I could get a little kinky. Perhaps, I should bring them out and start using them on you."

"Oh yes, let me see."

Adam was fascinated by them.

"Oh yes, will you use these on me next weekend?"

"Sure, but why not now or during the week?"

"Because I want to explore some kinky sites on the web first and see what we can do with them."

It was too much for Peter so he grabbed his lover and took him back to bed, again.

"I don't think I have ever been so happy, Peter. It's going to hurt in a year's time, isn't it?"

Peter nodded his head and replied, "Unless we grow tired of each other, yes."

"I can't see that happening."

Since the mess deck in the barracks where the crew was billeted during refit was just a halfway house, no one took much notice if someone came in after work, showered, changed into civilian clothes, and disappeared until it was time for work the next day. In Adam's case, he didn't even do that. He quickly got to the point where he kept his work clothes at Peter's and the two of them went to work in uniform, ready to get straight to it. The dockyard police were civilians and were only interested in checking identities, not in worrying about a junior rating being in the same car as an officer everyday. The result was that Peter and Adam enjoyed their easy alliance.

The next weekend, Adam was almost bouncing off the walls when Peter brought out his kinky collection.

"Can I try all of these on you, Peter? Just to see how it all works."

Some serious kisses first then a shower, during which Adam said, "No messing around. I want you really horny when I become your master."

Peter couldn't let him get away with that and started tickling him. Adam had to leave the shower then.

"You wait until I have you restrained on the bed. You will pay for this."

Peter was putty in Adam's hands when they were all dried and stood naked in front of each other.

"I think you should be laid out on the bed on your back with your arms and legs spread wide."

Adam say, Peter do. Adam then used the ankle and wrist restraints to secure Peter in a star shape. Looking down on his lover, Adam's eyes watered a little.

'How can I be so lucky to have the love of this man? It's like a

dream come true. And even if I do only have him for one year, it will be worth it,' was his thought.

"I am going to make love to you for a little while before I punish you for seducing this poor innocent boy who was influenced by your seniority."

Giggles first, and then Adam sat on the bed and started on Peter, kisses on the lips to start and then those kisses moved down until they reached the nipples. Adam had never been in a position to play with those at his leisure so he spent an age licking, kissing, and finally grinding them between his teeth. Peter was gasping, this foreplay was so exciting. When he thought he would orgasm, Adam moved lower, spending another age licking and kissing Peter's cock and balls without taking any into his mouth. When he did eventually lift Peter's cock and slide his mouth over the glans before swabbing it with his tongue, Peter had an almighty orgasm, swamping Adam's mouth.

"You naughty boy, I didn't give you permission to cum. I shall have to punish you now."

Peter thought that was going to be interesting. How was he going to be punished while he was on his back?

Adam undid one of the leg-securing ropes and pulled it back to secure it to the same corner as the wrist, pulling it tight enough to force Peter to bend his leg until his knee was almost touching his shoulder. Adam did the same thing with the other one. The result, Peter was spread very wide with his arse some height off the bed. Adam put pillows under Peter's lower back so that he was comfortable and surveyed his handy work. The sight was so erotic it made Adam gasp. Peter's anus was on display at just the right height for him to kneel between Peter's legs and enter him. He stroked the cheeks as he spoke.

"This is such a pretty arse. It's a shame that I am going to have to beat it before I rape it."

Adam picked up the paddle and stood at the side of the bed. He brought the paddle down onto Peter's arse but watched his eyes. He didn't want to hurt his lover, just set up a sensuous tingle. He gave him ten. At the end, Peter's arse just had a little glow to it.

"Let that be a lesson to you, you sex maniac. Now, I am going to punish you even more."

With that, Adam was back on the bed and with a spit-slicked

finger gently finger-fucked Peter while he sucked him and played with his balls. Very soon, both of them were wandering around in space. Adam thought Peter was so sexy he could orgasm just playing with him.

"You have been such a naughty boy I am now going to see how many fingers I can get inside you."

Adam used proper lubricant because he wanted to make sure he definitely didn't make this uncomfortable for Peter. He did take very long to reach four fingers during which he managed to make Peter cum again. Now it was time for the big one. He lubricated his cock and slowly fed it all to Peter, once again watching his eyes. Fully embedded, Adam started slow-fucking his lover, noticing how quickly he came back to an erect state. Neither of them lasted long after that because Adam used his hands to play with Peter as he continued to fuck him. Adam's orgasm was so intense he passed out and fell onto Peter's torso.

Peter was quite concerned for a minute. He thought that if Adam was unconscious he would be unable to do anything. Doing this again, unless there was a third party appeared to be potentially quite dangerous. Adam came to quite quickly and Peter breathed a sigh of relief. Adam burst into tears.

"Oh, Peter, that was incredible."

Peter laughed with relief and pleasure.

"I know my love, but now I think you should untie me while I tell you something."

Adam did and Peter explained. Adam understood and was serious for a minute before his sense of humor cut in.

"Of course, you are right. If we do this in the future we must have David here, or Charlie and Chris, or why not all three and then we can have an orgy?"

Oh dear, what Pandora's Box that comment opened.

All cleaned up and laid alongside each other, Peter broached the subject.

"For a bit of raunchy fun, would you like us to have an orgy with the others?"

Adam had obviously been involved with group sex. That was how Peter had gotten involved with him in the first place, so he wasn't averse to the idea in principal.

"Mmm, the other twins are pretty sexy, aren't they? Charlie was the one who took my cherry when we joined the ship. That was when I realized I was going to be a bottom. David and I had blown each other and I always liked that, but being fucked was easily the best."

Adam laughed, watching Peter's eyes.

"I'm not really slutty, but I do like to be fucked when the person doing it is making love to me as well. Charlie and Chris always took their time and made it good for David and me. When you made love to me the first time though, I knew you were special. I don't know how I'm going to handle it when we have to part, Peter. I love you so much and in another year it is going to be so difficult to move on."

Adam was only saying what Peter was thinking. He thought that diversifying by having an orgy with the others might lighten the tension that was building between the two of them. If that went well, perhaps, just have one of the others with them a lot so that threesomes became the norm. The thought was interesting but Peter knew that wouldn't work for him really. He wanted Adam to himself.

Well, the orgy was fun. It took place one Saturday and by the time they called time, everyone had been fucked and sucked by someone else. It had all been light-hearted, Peter wanted it that way. The boys all slept where they could at Peter's that night, not wanting to go back to the barracks after such a fun day. The grins at breakfast pleased Peter. Without trying, he had brought the loyalty of these three boys forever. And more worryingly, a heightened love from Adam who had seen how gentle and loving Peter had been with his brother and the other twins.

Chapter 4

Nothing else happened during that year with Charlie, Chris, and David. Adam on the other hand was ashore every night and on weekends when he and Peter weren't required for duty. The love between the two of them just got deeper. When they had their leaves they went away together and came back to work glowing. Wherever they were abroad they felt safe to be themselves, and in places like Sitges they walked hand in hand reveling in their love. They played like kids on beaches in Thailand and Portugal, enjoyed long lazy dinners in open air restaurants, and made love several times every day. The Portugal trip was nearly their undoing.

Peter realized early in their relationship that Adam was happy in quiet rural settings. The bright lights and party atmosphere of the tourist resorts really weren't what he wanted. Peter found a little fishing village on the Portuguese coast between Lisbon and Oporto. It did have a casino complex but apart from that had a pleasant beach, a few pleasant restaurants and bars but wasn't touristy at all. He rented a self-catering apartment and was delighted when Adam saw it and almost buried Peter in kisses.

"Oh Peter, this is wonderful. How did you know I would like something like this?"

He was walking round the little apartment, looking at all the traditional furnishings and the view over the fishing port from the window in the sitting room.

"Can we come here and live? I won't even want to leave the apartment for anything."

Peter was so pleased he nearly cried with happiness.

The whole holiday was like that first few minutes. They arose early some mornings to go down to the harbor as the boats came in and bought fish for the day as it was unloaded. They went back to the apartment to make love before breakfast and then were off to the beach for lazy days in the sun, just happy to be with each other. On some nights, they would walk up to the casino, not to gamble, but to listen to the band and watch the cabaret before finding a local restaurant for dinner. The clientele, they found out, were nearly all from Coimbra, the large town inland. Other nights they would stay in the apartment and have romantic dinners, falling over each other in the tiny kitchen as they tried to cook dinner together, always with laughter and kisses.

Sometimes when they were out, they would forget themselves and move close to each other for a quick kiss: on the beach, in a bar, or restaurant, it didn't matter. When the mood took them they couldn't resist showing the other how much he was loved.

Neither of them said it, but returning to work from that leave was the biggest wrench of all for them. They might get in one more holiday like that before taking up new postings, but that would be it.

Lunch in the wardroom in the barracks on their first day back and Peter looked so sad most other officers avoided sitting with him, except the first lieutenant from his ship.

"Good leave, Peter?"

Peter tried to smile, but not very successfully.

"Yes Sir, the best ever."

"Why looking so glum then?"

"I think it may well have been the swan song for something that has been incredibly special in my life this last year, Sir."

"Yes, well, he is an incredibly handsome boy, isn't he?"

Peter nearly fell off his chair.

"Whatever do you mean, Sir?"

"My wife's sister married the local vet in Figueria da Foz in Portugal. We spent the holiday with them. We saw these two young men several times while we were there. They were quite patently very much in love. My wife couldn't stop looking at them whenever we saw them. 'Oh Colin, isn't that romantic? I don't think they have eyes for anyone else in the world,' was a comment she made several times. You obviously didn't, Peter, because we were quite close to you on several occasions."

Peter almost choked.

"So why haven't I been arrested, Sir?"

Colin Foster laughed, "Because I love my wife very much and if I had you and young Arnold arrested I am sure she would divorce me."

Peter didn't know what to say.

"I'm sorry, Peter. What are you going to do about young Arnold? You will both get new appointments in the next couple of months I imagine."

Peter shrugged and his eyes got quite damp.

"I don't know, Sir. You see, I do love him so much that I can shut the whole world out when I am with him."

Colin Foster knew about love. He had met his wife when he was a cadet at Dartmouth and had fallen in love with her like Peter had with Adam. The love had grown and matured into something wonderful. He couldn't conceive of hurting Peter or Adam for having the same kind of love, even though he had known in his long naval career that homosexuality was a court martial offence.

"Has young Arnold submitted a preference draft chit yet?"

Peter shook his head.

"Hold off on it. Where would you like to go when your new appointment comes up?"

Peter laughed a sick laugh, "The same ship as Adam."

Colin smiled, "That wouldn't be a good move unless it was a shore establishment, would it?"

Peter wasn't stupid, of course it wouldn't. At sea, there would be virtually nowhere to be together for loving sessions. They would almost certainly end up like the two sets of twins had, getting caught.

He shook his head feeling even more depressed now that the imminent parting had been brought up.

"I noticed all of your four communicators have passed for leading hand during refit. Good work on your part, Peter, for encouraging that. The skipper was saying how impressed he was with your performance as a divisional officer."

Peter wondered where this was going, and soon found out.

"If young Arnold put in his preference draft a request for a slot at Collingwood as Ship's Company, he might get it. One of my old classmates at Dartmouth is the appointer for Coms junior ranks, and I'm sure if I nudged him a little Arnold would get what he asked for. The skipper might talk to the officer's appointer as well and recommend you for a D.O. slot at Collingwood if you expressed a desire to instruct there."

Peter had to excuse himself for a minute. He almost ran from the wardroom to the nearest heads. He couldn't hold back the tears any longer at the thought of another two years with Adam. When he had calmed down, he mopped his eyes with loads of cold water to try to lose the puffiness before returning to the lunch table.

"Sorry about that, Sir."

"Not a problem, I'd get on to that this afternoon. Send it off straightaway and I'll have a word with my friend. You should get the heads up on that one within a couple of weeks. The moment you get confirmation make sure you mention to the skipper the next time you talk to him where you would like to go and why. I'll do the same."

"I'll owe you for the rest of my life if this comes off, Sir."

Colin laughed, "No you won't but you'll owe my wife. I'm sure if it comes off you will have to bring the young man to dinner before we sail for sea trials."

The wheels started churning. Peter told Adam the minimum amount of information just to get him to fill in the form correctly.

"If you get a shore establishment, Adam, it will give us a chance of some time together even if I get a ship."

That was good enough for Adam, but the tension was building now as the ship was prepared for sea trials. Both men knew they could be looking at just a couple of months before they moved. On the last month, they would almost certainly be at sea the whole time so there would be very limited chance for anything, not even a kiss.

A few days before they were to sail for Portland for sea trials, Peter and Adam packed their things ready to take everything back to the ship. Adam started crying jags at the flat. There was nothing Peter could do to calm him. He daren't mention the possibility of them being together for another two years because if it didn't happen it would make matters even worse. In truth, he was finding it difficult to hold it all together as well. David made matters worse for Peter, unintentionally, of course. He came to see Peter in his office.

"I'm really worried about Adam, Sir. He is talking about harming himself if you two are parted. I think he may be contemplating suicide."

Peter was stunned. He knew, of course, that Adam was very upset, but this was way beyond upset.

"I'm sorry, David, I'm not a lot better. You have no idea how much I love your brother."

"I think I do, Sir, I've seen it grow during the last year. Is there nothing you can do?"

Peter shook his head.

"I'm trying, but the chances of us both getting the same draft must be quite remote, even with the help I'm getting. He'll be with me every night until we go to sea, so I'll watch him. You, Charlie, and Chris must do the same during the day and when we get back to sea."

David nodded and left Peter, both of them feeling that life was running out of control for them all.

Peter went to see the first lieutenant after that conversation to see if he had any news.

"Oh yes, sorry Peter, I forgot. You should have young Arnold's posting before we go to sea. Jerry, my friend has confirmed it. He'll leave the ship when we complete sea trials, take one month's leave and then join Collingwood. I'll have another word with the skipper about you, but I daren't be too pushy otherwise he'll want to know why."

Peter was pleased that the effort was being made, but he was still skeptical that this could happen, and if it didn't he would be so worried about Adam he would probably be unable to function properly.

Two days later, Adam came to see Peter in his office and without any enthusiasm told him, "I'm going to Collingwood, Peter, two years shore-based. What about you?"

Peter shrugged.

"Nothing yet, logically I should get a shore base as well, but my seniority, or more precisely, lack of it, will probably swing it so that I go to sea again. Whatever happens, Adam, I'm going to love you forever and if we have to settle for just a few weeks a year, then so be it. I hate spending even one night away from you, but I'm not going to do anything silly because we have long spells apart."

Adam looked at him accusingly.

"David has been talking to you hasn't he?"

Peter replied, sounding a little up tight, "Of course, he has. He loves you very much as well. He is more a part of you than I am being your twin. We are both worried my darling boy. We knew this was going to happen. We have to work our way through this if we are to have a future together."

It was too much for Adam. He threw himself into Peter's arms and sobbed.

"But two years is such a long time. I can't stand it."

Peter stroked him and spoke gently to him, "Yes, it is. But if you do something silly, that is forever."

That shook Adam.

"Oh God, I promise I won't. I'll be so miserable, but I won't do anything stupid. I love you so much."

Sigh of relief from Peter, "And I love you so much as well."

The next day, Peter was summoned by the ship's tannoy to take an outside telephone call, "Lieutenant de Salis, speaking."

"Good morning, Lieutenant. This is Commander Winston. Your captain had a word with me. I have an appointment for you, but if you accept it you will have to lose a couple of weeks of your terminal leave from your present ship."

This sounded promising and Peter almost couldn't reply.

"That won't necessarily be a problem, Sir, depending on what it is."

"I have a new Coms officer ready to join you this week. That will give you a little over a month to hand things over to him. Then you can have two weeks leave and take a Divisional Officer and Instructor slot at Collingwood. I can hold the other leave over to the end of this new appointment so you won't lose it completely."

Peter wanted to crawl down the line and kiss this guy. He was laughing as he replied, "That is perfectly fine, Sir. I would love to accept the new appointment."

"Well done, Lieutenant. I'll get that off to you today."

Peter got out a thank you before the line went dead and then he hunted down the first lieutenant.

"If it wasn't totally inappropriate, Sir, I would kiss you. Adam and I have both been appointed to Collingwood."

Colin smiled and shook Peter's hand.

"You had better get young Arnold then and bring him to dinner at my house. Shall we say 1930 for 2000, casual, Peter. We don't want to frighten your boyfriend."

Peter almost floated on air as he sent for Adam.

"You sent for me, Sir?"

"Yes, come in Adam and close the door."

Door closed and Peter stood up and walked round his desk.

"Number one would like us to go to dinner tonight. His wife wants to meet the two lovers they saw in Portugal on their last holiday."

Of course, Peter had told Adam about it.

"If we both got Collingwood, she wanted to see us for dinner, so that's why we are going tonight."

It took a minute for Adam to register what Peter had said. He was so surprised at the invitation. Then it clicked.

"Oh my God," was all he got out before he totally disintegrated.

Through his sobs Adam managed to get out the few words that mattered.

"I'm never going to be this happy again in my life."

***

Peter had never met Ann Foster before but was not at all surprised that she was a vivacious and friendly person. Colin was such a terrific No.1 it was only to be expected. She was only a few years older than Peter but appeared much more mature and sophisticated. She made Adam feel totally at home and Peter could see him relax and start enjoying himself. He had eaten in good restaurants with Peter so when they sat down for what turned out to be quite a formal dinner, he was still relaxed.

"So, Peter, now that you are going to be with Adam for another two years, what are your plans?"

Peter laughed happily as he replied, "I've hardly had time to think about it. But I imagine it is time I bought a house, and the South Downs sounds like a good place to start. That will give us an easy commute into Collingwood every morning. I have hardly spent any money since I graduated so I can put down a sizeable deposit. I'll need a new car of course, but that's it. Adam will be a leading hand soon so he will have adequate spending money. I think we will manage very well."

"You don't think you'll have any problems then, Peter, bringing a rating into work with you every morning?"

Peter winced at that.

"I hope not, Sir. I'll probably have to drop him off outside the gate somewhere and let him walk in. I know that being seen with him socially is probably not on, but we are quite happy in our own world. If we want to go out we can always head further north from the house where other personnel are unlikely to go. We both love Traditional Jazz so we can head out to the bars on the Plain that have bands in them. I doubt many from Collingwood will get out there," then, looking at Ann he continued, "And on home ground, I doubt we will be kissing and holding hands like we did in Portugal."

Ann colored a little but laughed as she told Peter the truth.

"I thought that was wonderful. You two were so obviously in love it was romantic watching you. I just wish you could do that everywhere."

Colin just huffed as he joined the conversation.

"I'll probably be a retired Admiral before that happens, in or out of the service."

Peter looked at his No.1 and asked, "Have you got your new appointment yet, Sir?"

Colin smiled at all of them and then looked at his wife.

"I was going to leave it until we were alone, but as Peter has brought it up I might as well give you the bad news, Darling. I have another sea going commission. I am joining *H.M.S. Campdown* straight out of the build program."

Ann looked very disappointed until Colin grinned at her.

"Promoted Commander and given command of her. It will probably be a year before she is fitted out and ready for sea."

Ann cried, Peter nearly wrung Colin's hand off, and Adam just said quietly, "Congratulations, Sir."

"What a pity I don't get to pick my own crew, Peter. My new communications officer and leading telegraphist would've been the two people who are now sitting at my dinner table."

Both Peter and Adam expressed pleasure at that.

It was two happy young men that returned to their base that night, stopping to make out for a little while in a quiet lay by.

"The next month might be a little tense, Adam. We'll be at sea so no intimate contact. It would be silly to take any risks now that we have another two years together."

Adam nodded, knowing that it would still be difficult to be near Peter all the time but not be able to touch him.

The fates were still being kind to Peter and Adam during the shakedown trials. They spent quite a lot of time in Portsmouth letting specialists aboard to sort out problems found during the trials, allowing

Peter and Adam to get ashore house hunting. Before the problems were sorted, they had found a house that they loved. Set back off the main road about a 20 minute commute to Collingwood, it was in a cul de sac of only four houses. Peter checked with the estate agent to make sure none of the other three houses were occupied by naval personnel. They were also told there was no chain so they should be able to move in one month. That, of course, was perfect for them. They would move in together but Peter would only have two weeks leave against Adam's one month. They would still be together every night and on weekends if Peter didn't have a duty.

The day they left their ship in Plymouth after the work-up, they said goodbye to friends and fellow officers with an extra thank you to Colin, particularly, and headed for Fareham in the little car that had served Peter so well for the last year.

"Hotel tonight, estate agent for the keys first thing in the morning, shopping center to buy something to sleep on, a few more bits and pieces, and then home."

Adam hugged himself, *home*, that word sounded so good to him.

Making love that night in a hotel in Southampton had Adam crying with happiness. Peter took him round the planets several times.

"We are going to be able to do this almost every night for the next two years, my love. How does that sound?"

Adam had a grin nearly a mile wide. 'How could he be so lucky? What happens in two years' time? Who cares, two years is a long time when you are in your 20s.' They would be 27 and 21 when they had to go through this again and thinking about it now threatened to destroy the next two years.

Chapter 5

Peter frequently needed a rating to help him with his lectures and invariably used Adam. The pair became something of a double act that came to the notice of the captain. Peter didn't let the grass grow under his feet so he was right up to date in all aspects of communications as they were developed, invariably by defense-oriented civilian companies. Because they lived together, much of the new knowledge was communicated to Adam. In both cases their knowledge was outstripping their peers. They worked together very successfully for a year. Their love nest was the center of their lives. They seldom accepted invitations to go out with shipmates but always looked happy and contented.

At the end of that year, Peter had his annual meeting with his captain to receive his 206 form, which detailed the captain's opinion of his work.

"Come in, Peter, sit down."

Peter had only spoken to the captain when there was a wardroom reception he couldn't get out of, so he was wary at this very friendly approach.

"Thank you, Sir."

"How do you think your first year has gone?"

"I'm very happy in the job, Sir. I feel that I'm making a difference looking at passing out results. Being here also gives me the opportunity to keep ahead of the game with communications. The civilian companies developing Coms are always very cooperative when I have the time to go nosing around in their R&D departments."

The captain laughed.

"Yes, I've heard. What about the leading tel. who works with you? I've heard that his knowledge is beginning to embarrass his chiefs."

Peter blushed.

"Yes, I'm sorry about that, Sir, but the boy works with me so much that I pass my knowledge to him."

"Yes, well it's becoming a problem. He is too young to be promoted again and he doesn't have the qualifications for a commission so I am thinking of shunting him off to one of your Coms development companies in a liaison roll."

Peter's face fell and his shoulders slumped.

"You'll miss him, won't you?"

Peter looked shocked, not missed by the captain.

In a very shaky voice Peter replied, "I will be very sorry to lose him, Sir. Where do you think he will be sent?"

"There is a very hush-hush development unit on the North Wales coast. They have requested a senior communications officer and a rating to join them for liaison and development."

Peter realized this would be a terrific opportunity for Adam, but the thought of them being parted much earlier than originally planned made him sad.

"I will have my secretary draw up a request for your assessment of Arnold's capabilities and we'll send him off on a short leave before he has to become a temporary civilian."

Peter nodded. He was too upset to say anything else.

"Oh your 206, it's here and all I can say is I will be unhappy to lose you as well."

Peter looked at the captain, completely bemused by that comment.

"I'm sorry, Sir. I don't understand."

"Well, I had to find a switched on officer for the appointment to Wales as well. It was really just between the two senior lieutenant commanders in your section, but then I bumped into Commander Foster the other day. He was a young lieutenant in my first command. We became good friends and despite the difference in our seniority at the time, it hasn't changed. He told me about a young Coms officer and a junior rating. He appeared to be very concerned about what happens to them. Just make sure you don't let me down and look after young Arnold."

Peter was close to tears as he looked at the smug expression on the captain's face. He got up to leave feeling very shaky, and nearly fell over when the captain handed him his 206 and a memo that was headed, 'Legalization of Homosexuality.'

He managed a 'thank you, Sir,' before leaving.

Once outside the office, he read the memo. It was official. Homosexuality would no longer be an offence against naval discipline. Peter couldn't hide it as he left the admin block. The tears were streaming down his face.

Adam was going crazy when he saw Peter. The puffy eyes gave away the fact that he had been crying.

"What is it, Lover?"

Peter handed him the memo and told him, "You are going to become a civilian effectively and move to North Wales."

Adam was about to open the waterworks when Peter continued, "And I'm going with you to make sure you behave yourself."

Two very happy men drove home that day and Peter told Adam that once again Colin Foster had a hand in their good luck.

That night, Peter wrote a long thank you letter to Colin before thinking about the write up he would be doing on Adam the next day.

The outcome of all the paperwork was Peter and Adam receiving new appointments as liaison with defense contractors. The detail was even more thrilling for both of them. If they were found to be satisfactory to the companies they liaised with, the appointments would be for five years.

The love nest would be rented out for extra income. Their accommodation at their new appointments would be at the expense of the contractor and both of their salaries would be enhanced for civilian postings. All round the five years would mean that they saved a lot of money, lived together, and spent their working life in civilian clothes. Peter intended to tutor Adam for his next promotion but his long-term thinking was that when this appointment ended he hoped his reputation would be made so he could resign from his commission to work as a civilian with one of the companies, and Adam could buy out his contract and do the same. Despite homosexuality being legal in the services now, Peter was convinced that they would be let go without any hassle because of the rank differences. An officer and a rating in a relationship would be frowned on.

For Adam, life got even better soon after they arrived in Carmarthen. David was reappointed to the Naval Recruitment office in Cardiff. The twins would now be able to see each other almost every week if they wanted to.

Peter and Adam had plenty to be amused about when they arrived at their new appointments. They went straight to see the personnel manager who looked a little embarrassed.

"Lt. de Salis and Mr. Arnold, welcome to Marathon Communications. This is our first service liaison appointments and we have only just been made aware of the social difference between a commissioned officer and a rating. We understand that it is not acceptable in the service for you two to live in the same accommodation. Unfortunately, we have already commandeered a very nice, two-bedroom house for you. If you will bear with us for a few days we'll slip one of you into a hotel until we can find another flat or house."

Peter beamed at this very nice man, as he thought of him.

"That won't be necessary. I have worked with Adam for nearly two years now and will be quite happy to share with him as long as we are here."

The manager was pleased because unnecessary expense was avoided and he thought that this naval officer wasn't going to be one of those snotty types.

They settled in quickly doing what they had done before, work with communications equipment, except that now it was all state of the art, high-tech equipment in development. Peter was kept at the pointed end because he was expected to report to the Admiralty on the progress of different equipment. Adam worked further down the line on testing, but both of them were gaining huge amounts of knowledge beyond what they would get in the navy.

It didn't take the management long to realize that these two naval people were in a relationship. Whenever they were together they almost glowed with the pleasure of each other's company. Invitations to social events came addressed to both of them. Civilians weren't fussy about rank differences.

David drove up for the weekend when he was free and the three of them went exploring. The first night, Adam looked at Peter before bedtime and made a suggestion that was a prelude to a load of fun.

"David and I always slept together as we grew up, Peter. Will you be terribly upset if we do that tonight? It will be so nice to cuddle my brother again."

Peter looked at these two beautiful young men, not yet 20 years old.

"Mmm, two for the price of one, I think I can handle that."

He was laughing as he spoke and that confused Adam.

"I wasn't suggesting an orgy, Peter."

Still grinning, Peter came back at him, "I wasn't either, my lovely boy. But I have been to bed with David before and I know you two have played as well. If you want us to play, I'm just saying I wouldn't be upset. You know how much I love you, I think I have some to spare for your double."

Adam and David looked at each other and grinned, thinking about the first time they experienced a love in with Peter.

"Ok, but I'm sleeping in the middle," Adam grinned and continued, "You'll have to crawl over me to get to David."

"Or both of us will just have to attack you."

"Oh yes please, can we do that?"

Much laughter and the twins noticed Peter getting an erection. A nod from Adam and the two of them got on either side of Peter and in no time had him stripped naked.

"Perhaps, we should both attack you instead."

Peter wasn't going to protest that one and soon had the boys together in their bedroom, stripping them very erotically. The only way that Peter could tell them apart when they were naked was their hairstyle. Adam's hair was longer, not being under naval discipline like David. Three seriously erect penises needed satisfying and the twins were put to action. Peter was in the middle on the bed with Adam and David playing with him. He was in heaven, being able to play with both of them as they played with him.

David swiveled round to blow Peter and that allowed Peter to blow him. Adam sat up to watch initially before stroking Peter's body then moved to stroke his brother.

"I love you both so much. I'm so pleased we can do this."

Peter came off David and vice versa and as if they had programmed it, pulled Adam down between them and David started blowing Adam while Peter buried his boy in kisses and caresses. Eventually, David and Adam were 69ing while Peter started working on David's bottom. Peter slowly opened him up until he thought David was ready. He then lubed them both and slid into David. The boy was so relaxed that Peter was able to go all the way. Adam could watch from such close quarters that the eroticism made him blow his load into his brother's throat very soon after Peter entered him. He remained in the same position though, allowing David to continue sucking him as he continued sucking his brother, while Peter fucked him to orgasm.

Three very satisfied young men cleaned up and fell back into bed, with Adam in the middle being spooned by Peter and David being spooned by his brother.

Adam was probably the happiest young man in the world the next morning. It was the first time he had seen his brother in a year and the meeting had resulted in a love in that he could only have imagined prior to this.

"I love you so much for letting us love in last night."

"And I just love you so much I could refuse you nothing."

David took it all in and looked between his brother and Peter. The happiness that they shared pleased him immensely, but at the same time made him a little sad. It would be so nice to have a proper boyfriend like Adam.

Successful weekend, David returned to Cardiff after telling his brother that he worked most weekends so they wouldn't be able to do this very often.

Peter tried to lighten the atmosphere by joking.

"Well, that is probably a good thing. Having one beautiful boy to make love to keeps me almost exhausted, two of you frequently would probably put me in a hospital. But it was lovely to see you again, David. Don't be a stranger, will you?"

David was happy with the invitation and left his brother, quite happy with his weekend.

"I love you so much, Adam, that I have never delved into your past. What is the situation with your parents?"

Adam blushed.

"I'm sorry, Peter. I have been very negligent there. They are both alive and I haven't been to see them since I left training. I talk to them sometimes on the phone and David goes home for most of his leave. He tells them that I have a greater commitment to the navy because of my job. We ought to go see them soon so that I can introduce them to the man I love. It will be a shock to them, I expect. David will probably come out to them at the same time."

"How do you think they will take it?"

Adam looked sad as he replied, "I don't think they will be very happy so we may have to leave straightaway. What about yours?"

"They rejected me when I told them while I was at university. It just made me work harder and that paid off with my second appointment to Dainty as senior Coms officer, where I met you."

Peter thought they ought to get the meeting out of the way as soon as possible and engineered a weekend off the same time as David's so that all three of them would confront the parents together.

The rejection didn't happen. Mark and Maria Arnold were not best pleased that they had beautiful twins that were both gay.

"I have heard all the talk about the gay gene, so I can only assume that neither of you had any choice in your sexuality. You must be the same, Peter, so I hope you will look after my sons."

"I'm certainly doing all I can to look after Adam, Sir. David is more difficult because he is not with us or in my field of influence."

"I'm sure I can rely on Peter's help if I ever need it, Dad, and we do see each other when I have a weekend free."

That appeared to satisfy the parents and after a little maneuvering, Peter and Adam had a bedroom and David a separate one. It didn't stop him sliding into Peter and Adam's room for cuddles before they slept.

Peter understood Adam's love of the quiet rural areas after that weekend. His home was in a sleepy little market town. It was quaint and felt a lot like they had slid back in time.

"The bright lights didn't entice you as you grew up then, Adam?"

Both twins laughed as they recounted a foray into the big city when they were sixteen and were besieged by other gay young men.

"It was pretty frightening because at that time, David and I hadn't sorted our sexuality. Before we joined the navy we did though, and when we met Chris and Charlie we soon expanded it and became happy bottoms to their big cocks."

"Sluts," said Peter as they laughed together.

Life was good. Occasional visits to parents, sometimes with David kept both boys happy.

David's appointment ended and he went to Collingwood for a course before getting another sea appointment. He shared his leave between his parents and Peter and Adam's house. For the next two years,

Peter and Adam just had each other to worry about. They made love almost every day and grew into their jobs with the R&D Company.

David came home and took up a similar job at Collingwood that Adam had done before, but now he was working towards his next promotion, helped enormously by Peter and Adam.

Two more years and David received his promotion making him the youngest Petty Officer in the Royal Navy in his specialization. Peter wanted to know what to expect within the next year for himself and Adam. First stop was the head of R&D with the company.

"Come in, Peter. You must be a mind reader. I was going to send for you today. You and Adam have less than a year to do of the five that we contracted for. What are you going to do now?"

"I was going to find out from you what you wanted and then talk to the navy appointers."

"Quite honestly, Peter. We would like to keep you. The liaison job will remain, I expect, but we would like you to join our company. Your degree and your experience with us could put you in as the head of a development team. If you can get a release from the navy, I can offer you a contract which would double your salary."

Peter was stunned. He had no idea he was that good. Obviously, his leadership training as an officer was a boon, but he was reserved enough about his own abilities to not realize he was good.

"That is an extremely generous offer, Sir. I know I should jump at it, but I need to see what I can do for Adam Arnold before I make a decision."

"Yes, well we are all quite aware of your relationship which is why I have an offer for Adam, if he can get out of the navy too. We would be prepared to put our weight behind any attempt you can make to get release for both of you."

Peter was seriously surprised and it showed on his face.

"Come along, Peter, you must have noticed that several of our whiz kids are gay. We actually practice positive discrimination because our gay employees are easily the most productive in the company."

Peter felt like such a fool. He was so wrapped up with his love for Adam he had never noticed other men of their sexuality.

"I'll get onto the navy today, Sir, and see what I have to do for Adam. I can resign my commission with just six months' notice as I have done the five years required to pay off my university funding. Adam may be able to buy himself out. He has only three years left on his engagement."

"Well, if a letter from us will help, know that it will be forthcoming."

That was it. Peter telephoned Colin's friend, who got Adam his Collingwood appointment and told him the story.

"Adam Arnold is actually an embarrassment to the navy now, Sir, because his knowledge outstrips even the Chief Tel. And he is too young and too junior to jump to a proper position for his knowledge."

"This is a little unusual, Lieutenant."

"I know, Sir. But the company would like him to stay here as well and I have been offered an appointment. Apparently, naval personnel rate highly with these people. You had better be careful who you send to replace us, Sir. You might lose them as well after five years."

Peter had said it as a joke, but the commander didn't see it that way.

"You had better tell Arnold to write a letter asking to buy out the remaining three years of his engagement and include a letter from the company laying out why we should release him as well."

The company must have put a load of pressure on the navy because it was only a few weeks later that Adam received details of how to terminate his navy career. He would remain on a naval appointment until his five years was completed and then he would be released at Collingwood. Peter resigned his commission at the same time and the two of them were sitting with personnel, thrashing out new contracts. Both ended with employment at salaries they could only have dreamt about in the navy.

Adam and Peter returned to Collingwood to complete their mustered out routine. They had to live on board because their house was still let, but now they could openly see each other without worry. One week later, they left in Peter's car to stay in a hotel for a couple of nights so that they could socialize with David.

"I have a new sea appointment, Far East for two years. I was told it was a married appointment based in Singapore at the High Commission, so someone slipped up. I could have gotten out of it but I told the appointer that I would be delighted to take it. I will have my own apartment so I should be able to have lots of fun with all those gorgeous Chinese and Malay boys."

Peter was so pleased. The appointment would stop Adam from worrying about his twin.

Back to North Wales and to their love nest. They were given six months to find their own home now that they were staff. That was no problem. They didn't even have to sell their home near Collingwood to obtain another mortgage and on their joint salaries, managed to buy an idyllic home set apart from other houses but still close to work. Another car was purchased for Adam who didn't always work the same hours as Peter.

They counted their anniversary as the first time they made love and celebrated the seventh soon after moving into their new home. They joked about the seven-year itch until Peter got serious.

"We work with some pretty fantastic guys, Lover. Aren't you ever tempted to try one?"

Adam looked aghast.

"Are you serious, Peter? I can't even begin to imagine my life without you. I would never go to bed with another guy unless we did it together like we do with David."

"I just wondered. I get so wrapped up in my work now I must come across as a bit of a nerd."

Adam laughed.

"Are you kidding? I still think you are the most exciting man on the planet. I have had seven years of incredible happiness with you. I still pinch myself occasionally to make sure I'm not dreaming. I also think about what might have been after you caught us with the other twins that night. My life could have been ruined, instead, look at what I have now."

What they had was a life together. David continued to serve in the Royal Navy, telling Peter and Adam that he had decided to marry it. He remained there to his retirement as a lieutenant commander, having taken a general duties commission when he became a Chief Tel.

And the Watson's, well, Chris and Charlie served to 27, left the navy then became male models making a fortune with top fashion houses. Their incredible bodies were their passports to modeling underwear and then doing sexy adverts for men's toiletries, usually with a woman wrapped around them that always amused the others.

All of them managed to meet occasionally when David was in the UK. The tales Chris and Charlie told about their sex lives were a continuing source of amusement.

This story should have started with, 'Once Upon a Time,' because it definitely ended, 'Happily Ever After.'

The End

Here is a sample from another story you may enjoy:

NAUGHTY GAY EROTICA

PLAY
& Pretend

DEXTER CHASE

Jack had been watching Evan for weeks at the start of the new soccer season. Mostly, the observation was carried out in the locker and shower rooms after football practice. Evan was the new boy, started at the beginning of year eleven, but a year older than most. Jack had befriended him from the start, but not purely for altruistic reasons. To Jack's eyes, Evan was simply gorgeous.

The girls had started to swarm round him like bees round a honey pot, but he never hitched up with one of them. Jack thought that was very strange, and started his observation campaign. He noted that Evan was nearly always first in the shower, and chose the shower head in the corner that allowed him to keep his genitals hidden, if he wanted to, but able to scope out everyone else in the showers. He was nearly always last out and, once again, Jack noted why. Evan sported a very chubby cock, not quite erect, so he obviously had learnt to control it.

When Jack was convinced that Evan's actions weren't accidental, he followed suit and arrived in the showers in time to see Evan's cock completely flaccid. It was still an impressive size, confirming in Jack's mind that it would grow into a monster. He waited on one occasion until the locker room was nearly empty before approaching Evan.

"Quite a few impressive pieces of equipment, don't you think, Evan?"

Evan blushed, and couldn't look directly at Jack.

"What do you mean?"

"Come on Ev, I've seen you scope out the guys. You must know, to the millimeter, the length of every flaccid cock in the first and second elevens."

Evan vehemently denied it.

"That denial doesn't wash buddy; I've watched you for too long. You must know, by now, that yours is the longest, by quite a lot. If you are a grower and not a shower, it is probably a ten-incher, which is pretty impressive."

Evan was pleased with that comment, and impressed with Jack's accuracy. He was almost exactly ten inches, and he was very proud of it.

They finished dressing and left the locker room to head home. Jack knew that they only lived one road apart, so to Evan's surprise, Jack stuck with him.

"Do you live this way, Jack?"

"Yeah, Moscow Road."

"I only live one road beyond... in Crimea Crescent."

"Really? Would you like to drop off at my house for a while? We could do our assignments together and then have a talk."

Evan smelled a rat.

"What do you want to talk about?"

"Oh, nothing much: school, soccer, how you're fitting in as the new boy."

Evan shrugged, "Ok."

The first bit went fine; doing assignments together worked well, because two brains were better than one.

Jack got up from his chair and stretched, before removing his shirt and tie. Then he toed off his shoes and bent to take off his socks. When he stood up, he undid his belt, undid the button at the waist, and pulled down the zip, slipping the trousers over his hips, dropping them to the floor and, again, bending to pick them up, but this time with his back to Evan. Through his legs, he saw Evan's eyes looking at his butt.

After he had hung the trousers, he sat back down making sure that by slipping down on the chair it forced his boxers up tight in his crotch, clearly outlining his cock down his left leg. Again, Evan's eyes looked at the display before looking up at Jack and blushing, realizing he had been caught.

"See something you like, Ev?"

Evan gulped and then tried to brazen it out.

"Not really; just wondering why you have stripped off."

"I like to be comfortable when I'm chilling out in my room. Besides, mum and dad won't be in for another couple of hours, so I get to beat off in comfort without worrying about being disturbed."

While he was talking, Jack had been stroking his cock through his boxers, and it had grown considerably, and continued to grow when he put his hands behind his head. Evan gulped, and looked very uncomfortable as he kept taking quick glances at the growing appendage.

He tried to adjust his own growing cock without Jack noticing, and failed completely.

"Now I think you see something that you like, and it's got you all excited."

If you enjoyed this sample, look for **Play & Pretend**.

From the Author

If you enjoyed any of my books then please share the love and click like on my books in Amazon.

If you write me a review and send me an email I will send you a free book, or many.
(Just know that these emails are filtered by my publisher.)

Good news is always welcome.

One Last Thing, For Kindle Readers...

When you turn the page, Kindle will give you the opportunity to rate this book and share your thoughts on Facebook and Twitter. If you enjoyed my writings, would you please take a few seconds to let your friends know about it? Because... when they enjoy they will be grateful to you and so will I.

Thank You!

Dexter Chase
dexter_chase@awesomeauthors.org

About the Author

Dexter Chase is a writer of hot, gay erotica stories in both paperback and Kindle versions.

His very first book published is **Mastered (Sensual Tales from Ancient Egypt)** which is about an eighteen-year old Ajax, who was taken as a slave and brought to a great house by a high-ranking soldier.

Check out his books and you'll enjoy extreme gay erotica of all time.

www.ingramcontent.com/pod-product-compliance
Lightning Source LLC
Chambersburg PA
ЧW070944200626
11CB00025B/1537